Confessions
of an Ugly
Stepsister

Also by GREGORY MAGUIRE

Wicked:
The Life and Times
of the Wicked Witch of the West

Confessions of an Ugly Stepsister

GREGORY MAGUIRE

ILLUSTRATIONS BY BILL SANDERSON

ReganBooks

An Imprint of HarperCollins*Publishers*

HarperCollins books may be purchased for educational, business, or sales promotional use. For information please write: Special Markets Department, HarperCollins Publishers, Inc., 10 East 53rd Street, New York, NY 10022.

FIRST EDITION
Designed by Joseph Rutt

ISBN: 0-06-039282-7

00 01 02 03 ❖/RRD 10 9 8 7 6 5 4

For Andy Newman

If I could say to you, and make it stick,
A girl in a red hat, a woman in blue
Reading a letter, a lady weighing gold . . .
If I could say this to you so you saw,
And knew, and agreed that this is how it was
In a lost city across the sea of years,
I think we should be for one moment happy
In the great reckoning of those little rooms . . .

> —Howard Nemerov, "Vermeer,"
> from *Trying Conclusions:*
> *Old and New Poems*

CONTENTS

For artist residencies during which parts of this book germinated and were written, the author would like to thank the Isabella Stewart Gardner Museum in Boston, Blue Mountain Center in upstate New York, the Hambidge Center in northern Georgia, and the Virginia Center for the Creative Arts.

Stories Painted on Porcelain

Hobbling home under a mackerel sky, I came upon a group of children. They were tossing their toys in the air, by turns telling a story and acting it too. A play about a pretty girl who was scorned by her two stepsisters. In distress, the child disguised herself to go to a ball. There, the great turnabout: She met a prince who adored her and romanced her. Her happiness eclipsed the plight of her stepsisters, whose ugliness was the cause of high merriment.

I listened without being observed, for the aged are often invisible to the young.

I thought: How like some ancient story this all sounds. Have these children overheard their grandparents revisiting some dusty gossip about me and my kin, and are the little ones turning it into a household tale of magic? Full of fanciful touches: glass slippers, a fairy godmother? Or are the children dressing themselves in some older gospel, which my family saga resembles only by accident?

In the lives of children, pumpkins can turn into coaches, mice and rats into human beings. When we grow up, we learn that it's far more common for human beings to turn into rats.

Nothing in my childhood was charming. What fortune attended our lives was courtesy of jealousy, greed, and murder. And nothing in my childhood was charmed. Or not that I could see at the time. If magic was present, it moved under the skin of the world, beneath the ability of human eyes to catch sight of it.

Besides, what kind of magic is that, if it can't be seen?

Maybe all gap-toothed crones recognize themselves in children at play. Still, in our time we girls rarely cavorted in the streets! Not hoydens, we!—more like grave novices at an abbey. I can conjure up a very apt proof. I can peer at it as if at a painting, through the rheumy apparatus of the mind . . .

. . . In a chamber, three girls, sisters of a sort, are bending over a crate. The lid has been set aside, and we are digging in the packing. The top layer is a scatter of pine boughs. Though they've traveled so far, the needles still give off a spice of China, where the shipment originated. We hiss and recoil—*ughh!* Dung-colored bugs, from somewhere along the Silk Route, have nested and multiplied while the ship trundled northward across the high road of the sea.

But the bugs don't stop us. We're hoping to find bulbs for planting, for even we girls have caught the fever. We're eager for those oniony hearts that promise the tulip blossoms. Is this is the wrong crate? Under the needles, only a stack of heavy porcelain plates. Each one is wrapped in a coarse cloth, with more branches laid between. The top plate—the first one—hasn't survived the trip intact. It has shattered in three.

We each take a part. How children love the broken thing! And a puzzle is for the piecing together, especially for the young, who still believe it can be done.

Adult hands begin to remove the rest of the valuable Ming dinnerware, as if in our impatience for the bulbs we girls have shattered the top plate. We wander aside, into the daylight—paint the daylight of childhood a creamy flaxen color—three girls at a window. The edges of the disk scrape chalkily as we join them. We think the picture on this plate tells a story, but its figures are obscure. Here the blue line is blurred, here it is sharp as a pig's bristle. Is this a story of two people, or three, or four? We study the full effect.

Were I a painter, able to preserve a day of my life in oils and light, this is the picture I would paint: three thoughtful girls with a broken plate. Each piece telling part of a story. In truth, we were ordinary children, no calmer than most. A moment later, we were probably squabbling, sulking over the missing flower bulbs. Noisy as the little ones I observed today. But let me remember what I choose. Put two of the girls in shadow, where they belong, and let light spill over the third. Our tulip, our Clara.

Clara was the prettiest child, but was her life the prettiest tale?

Caspar listens to my recital, but my quavery voice has learned to speak bravely too late to change the story. Let him make of it what he will. Caspar knows how to coax the alphabet out of an inky quill. He can commit my tale to paper if he wants. Words haven't been my particular strength. What did I see all my life but pictures?—and who ever taught the likes of me to write?

Now in these shriveled days, when light is not as full as it used to be, the luxury of imported china is long gone. We sip out of clay bowls, and when they crack we throw them on the back heap, to be buried by oak leaves. All green things brown. I hear the youthful story of our family played by children in the streets, and I come home muttering. Caspar reminds me that Clara, our Clara, our Cindergirl, is dead.

He says it to me kindly, requiring this old head to recall the *now*. But old heads are more supple at recalling the past.

There are one or two windows into those far-off days. You have seen them—the windows of canvas that painters work on so we can look through. Though I can't paint it, I can see it in my heart: a square of linen that can remember an afternoon of relative happiness. Creamy flaxen light, the blue and ivory of porcelain. Girls believing in the promise of blossoms.

It isn't much, but it still makes me catch my breath. Bless the artists who saved these things for us. Don't fault their memory or their choice of subject. Immortality is a chancy thing; it cannot be promised or earned. Perhaps it cannot even be identified for what it is. Indeed, were Cinderling to return from the dead, would she even recognize herself, in any portrait on a wall, in a figure painted on a plate, in any nursery game or fireside story?

I

THE OBSCURE CHILD

Marketplace

The wind being fierce and the tides unobliging, the ship from Harwich has a slow time of it. Timbers creak, sails snap as the vessel lurches up the brown river to the quay. It arrives later than expected, the bright finish to a cloudy afternoon. The travelers clamber out, eager for water to freshen their mouths. Among them are a strict-stemmed woman and two daughters.

The woman is bad-tempered because she's terrified. The last of her coin has gone to pay the passage. For two days, only the charity of fellow travelers has kept her and her girls from hunger. If you can call it charity—a hard crust of bread, a rind of old cheese to gnaw. And then brought back up as gorge, thanks to the heaving sea. The mother has had to turn her face from it. Shame has a dreadful smell.

So mother and daughters stumble, taking a moment to find their footing on the quay. The sun rolls westward, the light falls lengthwise, the foreigners step into their shadows. The street is splotched with puddles from an earlier cloudburst.

The younger girl leads the older one. They are timid and eager. Are they stepping into a country of tales, wonders the younger girl. Is this new land a place where magic really happens? Not in cloaks of darkness as in England, but in light of day? How is this new world complected?

"Don't gawk, Iris. Don't lose yourself in fancy. And keep up," says the woman. "It won't do to arrive at Grandfather's house after dark. He might bar himself against robbers and rogues, not daring to open the doors and shutters till morning. Ruth, move your lazy limbs for once. Grandfather's house is beyond the marketplace, that much I remember being told. We'll get nearer, we'll ask."

"Mama, Ruth is tired," says the younger daughter, "she hasn't eaten much nor slept well. We're coming as fast as we can."

"Don't apologize, it wastes your breath. Just mend your ways and watch your tongue," says the mother. "Do you think I don't have enough on my mind?"

"Yes, of course," agrees the younger daughter, by rote, "it's just that Ruth—"

"You're always gnawing the same bone. Let Ruth speak for herself if she wants to complain."

But Ruth won't speak for herself. So they move up the street, along a shallow incline, between step-gabled brick houses. The small windowpanes, still unshuttered at this hour, pick up a late-afternoon shine. The stoops are scrubbed, the streets swept of manure and leaves and dirt. A smell of afternoon baking lifts from hidden kitchen yards. It awakens both hunger and hope. "Pies grow on their roofs in this town," the mother says. "That'll mean a welcome for us at Grandfather's. Surely. Surely. Now is the market this way?—for beyond that we'll find his house—or that way?"

"Oh, the market," says a croaky old dame, half hidden in the gloom of a doorway, "what you can buy there, and what you can sell!" The younger daughter screws herself around: Is this the voice of a wise woman, a fairy crone to help them?

"Tell me the way," says the mother, peering.

"You tell your own way," says the dame, and disappears. Nothing there but the shadow of her voice.

"Stingy with directions? Then stingy with charity too?" The mother squares her shoulders. "There's a church steeple. The market must be nearby. Come."

At the end of a lane the marketplace opens before them. The stalls are nested on the edges of a broad square, a church looming over one end and a government house opposite. Houses of prosperous people, shoulder to shoulder. All the buildings stand up straight—not like the slumped timber-framed cottage back in England, back home . . .

—the cottage now abandoned . . . abandoned in a storm of poundings at the shutters, of shouts: "A knife to your throat! You'll swallow my sharp blade. Open up!". . . Abandoned, as mother and daughters scrambled through a side window, a cudgel splintering the very door—

Screeeee—an airborne alarm. Seagulls make arabesques near the front of the church, being kept from the fish tables by a couple of tired, zealous dogs. The public space is cold from the ocean wind, but it is lit rosy and golden, from sun on brick and stone. Anything might happen here, thinks the younger girl. Anything! Even, maybe, something *good.*

The market: near the end of its day. Smelling of tired vegetables, strong fish, smoking embers, earth on the roots of parsnips and cabbages. The habit of hunger is a hard one to master. The girls gasp. They are ravenous.

Fish laid to serry like roofing tiles, glinting in their own oils. Gourds and marrows. Apples, golden, red, green. Tumbles of grapes, some already jellying in their split skins. Cheeses coated with bone-hard wax, or caught in webbing and dripping whitely—cats sprawl beneath like Ottoman pashas, open-mouthed. "Oh," says the younger sister when the older one has stopped to gape at the abundance. "Mama, a throwaway scrap for us! There must be."

The mother's face draws even more closed than usual. "I won't have us seen to be begging on our first afternoon here," she hisses. "Iris, don't show such hunger in your eyes. Your greed betrays you."

"We haven't eaten a real pasty since England, Mama! When are we going to eat again? Ever?"

"We saw few gestures of charity for us there, and I won't ask for charity here," says the mother. "We are gone from England, Iris, escaped with our lives. You're hungry? Eat the air, drink the light. Food will follow. Hold your chin high and keep your pride."

But Iris's hunger—a new one for her—is for the look of things as much as for the taste of them. Ever since the sudden flight from England . . .

—running along the shadowed track, panting with pain in the chest, tumbling into a boat in the darkness—running, with the fear of hobgoblins at their heels. Imps, thwarties, grinning like demons, hungry to nip their ankles and sip their blood—

And what if an imp has secreted itself in the Harwich ship and follows like a skulking dog, to pester them in this new land all over again?

To keep from a panic, Iris says to herself: *Look at how things are, look: there, there, there. . . . We are someplace new, someplace else, safer.*

Ruth stops. She is older than Iris, a solid thing, already more than normal adult size, but simple. A pendulum of spit swings out and makes a tassel. Iris reaches and wipes Ruth's mouth. Ruth has a set of shoulders that would grace an ox, but she doesn't have an ox's patience. Her brown eyes blink. She lunges toward the nearest rack of produce, a tray heaped with sun-spotted early pears.

"No, Ruth," says the mother, and pulls her back.

Iris has a sudden notion of how she and her family must look, as stolid Englishers. Englishers in this European other-world, with its close, rich hills of architecture. The lumpy Fisher family, traipsing like oafs on a pilgrimage: —The spiky mother, Margarethe, tugging at her gigantic firstborn. —Ruth, heaving her lungs like a bellows, working up to a wail. —And Iris herself, gaunt and unlovely as a hermit, shrinking into herself as best she can.

The men of the market duck their heads to keep from

watching a woman's woes. The wives of the market, however, stare and don't give any ground. No one offers a bruised apple or a smallish pear to calm Ruth or to make Margarethe's plight easier. The market women tuck their hands in apron pockets to mind their small clutches of coins. There's no habit of charity here, at least not for the ugly foreigner.

Strong Ruth is less pliant than usual. She nearly succeeds in breaking out of her mother's grip. Margarethe, sorely tried, pitches her voice low. "Ruth! God's mercy, that I'm harnessed to such a beast! Give way, you willful thing, or I'll beat you when we get to Grandfather's. In a strange place, and no one to wipe your eyes then, for I'll keep Iris from cozening you!"

Though slow, Ruth is a good daughter. Today, however, hunger rules her. She can't break from Margarethe's hold, but she kicks out and catches the corner of the rickety table on which the pears are piled. The vendor curses and dives, too late. The pears fall and roll in gimpy circles. Other women laugh, but uneasily, afraid that this big little girl will overturn their displays. "Mind your cow!" barks the vendor, scrabbling on her hands and knees.

Margarethe looses a hand toward Ruth's face, but Ruth is twisting too fast. She backs up, away from the stall, against the front wall of a house. Margarethe's slap falls weakly, more sound than sting. She hits Ruth again, harder. Ruth's bleat mounts to a shriek, her head striking the bricks of the house.

A ground floor window in the house swings open, just next to Ruth. A treble voice rings out from within. It might be boy's or girl's. It's a word of exclamation—perhaps the child has seen Ruth topple the pears? Heads turn in the marketplace, while Ruth twists toward the young voice and Margarethe grabs a firmer hold. Iris finds herself scooping forward, pear-ward, while all eyes are elsewhere. In another moment she too has swiveled her head to look.

She sees a girl, perhaps a dozen years old, maybe a little more? It's hard to tell. The child is half hidden by a cloth hanging in the window, but a shaft of light catches her. The late afternoon light that gilds. The market stops cold at the sight of half the face of a girl in a starched collar, a smudge of fruit compote upon her cheek.

The girl has hair as fine as winter wheat; in the attention of the sun, it's almost painful to look at. Though too old for such nonsense, she clutches something for comfort or play. Her narrowed eyes, when she peers about the curtain's edge, are seen to be the blue of lapis lazuli or the strongest cornflower. Or like the old enamel that Iris saw once in a chapel ornament, its shine worn off prematurely. But the girl's eyes are cautious, or maybe depthless, as if they've been torn from the inside out by tiny needles and pins.

A woman's voice behind the child, coming from deep inside the house. The market is still. Why are the citizens so transfixed? "Clara?" says the inside voice.

Margarethe clamps Ruth's forearms tightly. The girl in the window cranes, watching Ruth shudder, judging Ruth's nonsense syllables. The girl leans over the windowsill, one curved forefinger at her plump lips. She looks at Ruth as a dog will look at a turtle—closely, without sympathy. "Are you a lost one?" she asks Ruth, and then says to Margarethe,

"Is she a changeling? Let her go if she is; let her go, and let's see what she'll do! Will she fly like a crow?"

"What kind of town is this, that the young address their elders with such nonsense?" cries Margarethe in competent Dutch, and the girl rears back for a moment, but the look of scrutiny doesn't vanish. Curiosity is too great.

Suddenly Ruth reaches up through the open window and takes hold of the girl's plaything—a small wooden windmill, with arms that pivot on a nail. Ruth puts the peg end of it in her mouth, by habit. She sucks as a new calf works at a teat. A dirty chuckle ripples through the crowd. But Ruth is calmed by the distraction, and Margarethe grips Ruth about the waist.

The blonde girl doesn't object. She leans forward, peering down at Ruth's face almost as if looking in a mirror. "Thing," says the girl, "oh, thing, *get away from here.*"

The onlookers watch warily. The girl's mother calls— "Clara!" And there is a flurry of action in the room. The girl is yanked back, the window slammed, the curtain closed.

Iris turns. Had they hoped to steal anonymously into this new place, they couldn't have done a worse job. Everyone in the town square is watching.

Margarethe squares her shoulders again and, without saying anything more, leads her daughters through to the other side of the market square. When they reach the far streets, where shadows have already thickened the day into an early dusk, Iris brings out the fruit she has snatched from the pavement. The pears are hard and juiceless. The three travelers munch them down to the pips, and eat the pips as well, and throw away the stems after sucking them dry.

The dusk is yielding to dark by the time they find Grandfather's house, in the lee of a city gate. There they learn that he has died a few years ago, and those who live inside are not family and have no obligation to take in the hungry strangers.

Stories Told Through Windows

A night spent huddled in the piss stink of an alehouse alley. Dogs chase them away at dawn. The mother and daughters brush the mud and straw off their only skirts, and walk toward the marketplace again to advertise for a position.

The mother's voice is calculating: by turns brassy, pious. Whatever works.

"I am Margarethe, Margarethe of the ten Broek family. My grandfather was Pieter ten Broek, who lived in the shadow of the Zijlpoort. A good family! I have come back here hoping to stay with them. But now I learn that he and his wife are dead, and my uncles are also lost though poxes and other whimsies of God. You don't know my face, but you know my grandfather's; he stood tall in this city. To honor his name, I ask you to stand by me, because there's no one left to turn to."

First, Margarethe makes her plea at the half doors of merchant halls. She'll do needlework in exchange for a clutch of blankets in a shed or byre. She'll do barn labor, just give her food for herself and her ungainly daughters. She'll mind the ill-tempered young, and she'll wring milk from her breasts if fractious infants need it. (Her breasts don't look up to the task.)

The merchants lob wilting lettuces at her.

So Margarethe turns to residential streets. Some of the houses are deafened, shutters like wooden muffs over their window-ears. Margarethe lingers in lanes till maids open up their masters' homes. She chatters with brave familiarity at the girls who come out to wash the stoops.

"Oh, you don't want to know what hardship we leave behind, in the godforsaken muck of an English country village. Bog stench to remember, I'll tell you now! But I was originally from here, one of you—my father left when I was still an infant, to Ely, to March, to teach the foolish English how to drain their damplands in the way we Hollanders perfected. He taught the trade to my husband, Jack Fisher, who performed it well enough . . . until the high tides of this fall. Then the earthworks were breached and the fens flooded and the fields and crops ruined beyond redemption. And the villagers of March and the web-footed fen folk could see what the coming winter would be like. They would rather have killed a Dutchman! But my father was dead of the ague, and no Dutchman was to be had, so they killed the next best thing: one of their own who had married a Dutch maid. My own husband, Jack."

A maid splashes a bucket of dirty water on the cobbles; Margarethe has to leap back to keep from a dunking.

A goodwife at a window, examining a stain in a lace collar.

Margarethe: "They cornered my man, my sorry Jack Fisher, out in a haunted copse one night last week! They hit my poor Jack on the head with an eel spear. My daughters and I left under cover of darkness the very same evening, fearing for our lives. English peasants are a vengeful lot, and we were seen as strangers, though the girls were born there."

. . . the sounds in the lane, of ale-courage and ale-anger, and the girls started from their sleep, and Margarethe's eyes darting, crusty; and her frightened voice: "We must get away from this place! Up, you lump-kin daughters, up!—or this sleep is your last!"—

The goodwife ducks her eyes away, as if Margarethe has been only a chirping jackdaw on the sill. The window shuts gently. Margarethe moves along to the window of a neighbor without losing the momentum of her recital.

"The English have a morbid fear of the foreigner among them! You know it! And though the girls have an English father, I trained them to speak the language of my grandfather, Pieter ten Broek, who served this town well, or so I am told. I thought we might need to return to our home soil, and so we have. We aren't wastrels or refugees. We're not dirty gypsies. We are your own. Welcome us back."

Iris sees that her mother isn't good at generating sympathy. Something about the hard edge of her jaw, the pinching nostrils.

"Look at my girls," says Margarethe. "If your stomach can bear it. Haven't I suffered enough?—with one of them gibbering and staggering like a drunken farmer on market day"—she shrugs at Ruth—"and the other"—she pushes Iris forward—"plain as a board, an affront to the eye? Why did God deny me sons, who might have been a comfort to a mother in distress? If we die on the streets of this town, for your coldness the hand of God will visit pestilence upon you! Good day. Bitch hound! Iris, mind your sister."

A palsied hand has reached out to draw the window closed against Margarethe and her daughters. A murmured prayer against Margarethe's curse.

"Let me tell you what I know about hunger and plague," says Margarethe, pestering a burgher who is trying to slide by her unaccosted. "Your townsmen refer us to the poor-houses here, and promise that the needy can fatten them-selves there on butter and beef. But I have seen the poor fight over a sick dog, to kill it and char its meat, and puke it up within the hour. I've known hunger to turn father against son, and husband against wife!"

"Mama, the things you say!" Iris is amazed at her moth-er's testimony.

"You think I embroider these things? Hunger is real," says Margarethe. "Haven't I seen children munching on rats?" But she softens her voice and tries a new approach.

"I have skills, old mother, I know the herbs and tisanes for the stiffness in the joints. I know what to gather, and how to dry it, and what to mete out, and what to reserve. I know the worts, the simples, the roots. I know"—she pauses, judg-ing her next audience of one weak-chinned old dame—"I know the holy words to pronounce, and when they fail, the unholy. I know the spells, I know the secret charms, I know the invisible comforts . . ."

The frightened crone bangs her shutter closed so hard that it nearly catches her crippled hand at the wrist.

"What we need is a table," says Iris, "a table that always groans with a weight of food, appearing by magic every day—"

"Fancy won't feed us, Iris," mutters Margarethe. "God's truth," she cries in anger, "is there no mercy in this damp town? Will the ill chance that chased us from England catch up with us at last, when we have no strength to keep running away?"

Midday. The sun doing its best, dragging its golden skirts through gritty streets. In a back lane, where the smells of the brewery get trapped in alleys and mildewy work yards, there is one window that doesn't swing shut. Margarethe stands, her hand pressed against her ribs, heaving, trying to keep from weeping with rage. At wit's end, she's working to invent a new story. Ruth plays with the pretty toy that the girl named Clara has thrust in her hands. Iris looks in the window.

The room is tall and airy, more stable than salon, an old storehouse for arms maybe. Iris peers. The room is in disarray. A table holds pots and mortars and grinding stones. A kettle of nose-wrinkling oil gently steams on a low fire. Paint-brushes brandish themselves out of clay pots, unruly as autumn bracken. Against the wall lean freestanding panels of wood, like a series of doors, and one or two panels are propped on easels in the center of the room. Every surface is worked over with color, fields of fog cut with strokes of unapologetic brightness. Every color that Iris has ever known, from midnight blue to the sourest citron.

A man turns, only slowly hearing Margarethe's words. He seems irritated to be yelled at through his own window, which has been opened for air and light, not for prying eyes or beggars on the prowl.

Iris leans farther to look. The consolation of gray, of green, the surprise of pink. The redemption of cloudy white on four new panels yet to be touched by image.

"Iris, don't be forward with the gentleman," murmurs Margarethe, readying her latest version of woe.

Iris ignores her mother. "What are you doing?" she says through the window.

Looking

The painter lays down a twig of red chalk and blows lightly on his fingertips. The folds of his clothes are lined with red as if powdered with the dust of bricks. He walks over to the window and shakes his head. "What kind of assault is this?" he grumbles.

"No assault, sir," cries Margarethe, now that she has caught one, reeling him in, "only a mother with hungry virgin daughters! What does the gentleman need to be done? A woman can be told to do anything. I can help a man's tired wife at all the household tasks. Tell me to sweep, to scrub; I will. Tell me to air a mattress, to fetch water from the well. I will. Tell me to kill a chicken?—I'll pluck it and stew it, send its feathers to the sack for pillowing, its blood organs to the pan for the company of onions, its bones thrown upon the dirt for the reading of fortunes."

"There's no wife here, or why would I be living in squalor? But hold your tongue while I think about it," he tells her, and he turns to glance at Ruth and Iris.

Ruth hides her eyes, but Iris looks right back at him. She

isn't looking for her father, no no; he is dead these seven days—

A voice outside the door as the door splinters: "And the husband is boxed on the head, bleeding into his bog, and we'll have his wicked wife next, and those girls!"—

—*Stay in the present moment. Look at the present moment.* She's just looking at a man who happens to be roughly her father's age. That's all.

He's a man of middle years, with an unshuttered light in his eyes. Iris doesn't remember seeing its like before. He strokes his gingery mustaches and draws fingers down a beard that needs hot water and the attention of a razor. His bald head is glazed from being in the sun without the black hat favored by prosperous burghers. His fingers are dyed with red and violet. Gingerbeard has calipers, scales, tools in his eyes; he stares at Iris. It's a look that's clean of human emotion, at least just now. He stares some sort of judgment at her. Iris drops her eyes at last, beaten by his attention.

"She will be of marriageable age within the month—" begins Margarethe. Iris winces.

"Silence," he murmurs, twitching his fingers at Margarethe.

And looks some more.

"This, then," he says at last. "There's a shed beyond where you can sleep a week or two, at least until my apprentice returns from his journeys on my behalf. After that we'll see. There's work to be done if you can live here in silence. You, Mother, will see to the needs of a bachelor's household. I won't name or number the tasks, but I want to eat and to sleep and to work without stopping when the mood arises. The older girl, can she wander about by herself?—there's a meadow not far from the bridge, just beyond the Amsterdamse Poort, where the new canal starts its journey to Amsterdam. The flowers of late summer grow there in abundance. She can collect them daily for my studio. The commonest weeds die within hours, and I need to look at them regularly. Is she capable of this? Good. Perhaps you—your name, your name in one word and no narrative—"

"Margarethe," she says, and lifts her head, "Margarethe Fisher, of the good Haarlem family ten Broek."

"Margarethe, if you attend, perhaps I can teach you to grind minerals for me and mix them with oil and powders, to make my colors."

"I am clever with grinding herbs and peppercorns and roots. Minerals and powders are as nothing to me."

"Good. And the girls, they are called—?"

"My elder daughter, Ruth, and the smart one, Iris."

"Not the usual Dutch names," he says, amused.

"They were born in the fens of Cambridgeshire. Their English father wasn't inclined to the names of saints and martyrs," says Margarethe, "so the choices were few. When we saw how our first child was spoiled, we named her Ruth, which I'm told means sorrow for one's own faults. Then we chose to name the next daughter Iris, with the hope it might encourage her to grow in beauty like a flower." She looks at Iris and her lips twitch. "As you can see, our hopes were badly abused."

"Iris is the smart one," he says.

"Smart enough for what you need, I'd guess." Is Margarethe leering a little? Surely not.

"For Iris, a difficult task," says Gingerbeard. "I'd like her to sit on a chair in the north light for hours at a time so I may observe her. She must sit without fidging, without speaking. She must keep her mouth shut. I will draw her in red chalk on parchment, and perhaps paint her if I'm pleased by my drawings."

Margarethe can't help herself. She says, "For what possible reason could you wish to render the likes of her?" Margarethe puts her hands on Iris's shoulder. The gesture is partly loving but partly a negotiation. And why not, Iris admits, when we can barely reach from one loaf to the next?

The painter replies, "My reasons are my own. Decide and answer me, for I have no more time for this right now. Tell me, yes or no."

"Your name, before we come in your door and accept your kind offer."

But he laughs. "My name can't seal a deal, my name doesn't increase the value of my canvases. My name has no place in a world in which Lucas Cranach and Memling and the Florentines show their paintings! Even in my own time I am anonymous, not quite known as the Master of the Dordrecht Altarpiece. That effort is much admired, but I'm not remembered as its creator. Just call me the Master, and my cock's pride will be assuaged. Will you enter or no?"

They troop inside. The smells in the studio are slightly offensive. Iris picks out the pungency of sappy, new-milled wood, the resin-scented oil, an eggy stink of sulfur, male sweat.

She stops hearing the clucking of her mother and the hulking shuffle of her sister. Iris looks at the works once her eyes have become accustomed to the inside light.

The panels are limned in red or black line. Some of them are worked with an olive or a sepia wash. A few have been taken further, the solid forms of human beings beginning to emerge from the gloom of the Master's preparations. Scraps of paper, scratched with silvery ink, are pinned to the edges of panels—sketches, she can see, of what the finished work might include.

The sketches are largely of people unclothed. Women and men alike.

Iris grabs her mother's hand and points wordlessly. Margarethe sets her jaw and considers the situation. At length she says, in a voice intended to be agreeable, "Master, is my daughter to sit undraped for you?"

"I am a painter, not a monster."

Eight or nine pieces in process, or pieces started and abandoned; Iris can't tell. Figures who are naked in the sketches appear clothed in the finished works.

Iris stares in distress at her mother. Behind the Master's back Margarethe makes a face at Iris that means: First we eat, *then* we refuse. Caution, daughter! But Margarethe goes on to remark, "We are in a Roman chapel, full of idols. In England few would sanction such blasphemy anymore. Does all of this painted beauty serve any purpose?"

"Who can say what purpose beauty serves? But at least the Roman Catholics used to pay well for work that inspires their devotions," says the Master, hunting through a pile of brushes for one to serve in the task at hand. "Back when the Roman Catholics were more than merely tolerated in this land."

"I see the Virgin in blue and scarlet; I see the Christ like a fat Dutch baby raised on cheese. I notice angels everywhere," says Margarethe dismissively.

"I paint my devils, dwarves, and depraved in a separate room," says the Master, waving a hand. "The door to which I keep locked. Not superstitious, I, but nor do I court the wrath of God any more than I need do."

Iris wants to ask: Do you paint imps, thwarties, sting-demons? The kind that run with soundless howling at the heels of mobs, egging them on? But she can't speak about this; her mouth won't collaborate with her mind.

Margarethe begins to arrange pots on the table in order of size. "Get on through to the house, don't handle my things," the Master says, "out back, go on! Be useful with pastry and broom and boiling water! Go to the marketplace and find a healthy fish for my dinner! Get out of my way!"

"What shall I use for coin, Master?" says Margarethe.

"My name," he says.

"The Master of Debt?" she says.

"Schoonmaker," he answered, "but the Master will do. It better do."

Margarethe straightens her spine. "Iris, attend your sister," she says. "You *are* the smart one. Enough of this mooning about, these vaporish sighs! Keep Ruth under your fist. Do you hear me?" Iris nods. "Reliable Iris," says Margarethe. "So off I go, and tonight we eat."

Iris keeps a hand on Ruth's shoulder till their mother has hurried out of sight. Then Iris continues her inspection. Since Iris doesn't speak, the Master doesn't seem to mind her being there. As he scrubs a patch of green to apply a yellow glow upon it, he mutters to her, or to himself. She listens as she wanders and looks.

He has a nice voice, rustly and gruff. "So your mother, like other small people, disapproves of sacred art! I should pack up my trunks and remove myself to the Spanish Netherlands, where a healthy Roman Catholic faith still requires a supply of religious imagery. But no, though the Calvinists here tolerate the Papist presence, even turning a blind eye to the secret chapels, the market for sacred art has disappeared."

Iris doesn't know or care about any of this.

"But seventy years ago? A hundred? Imagine this. Every eight miles found a clutch of houses with its own small church, and every church boasted a painting of the Holy Family. Jesus, Mary, and Joseph. The Gospels are peopled suddenly and forever by the images that artists deliver for you. We did our work, and God reaped the reward in increased prayer. The true consequence of beauty—tell your mother!—is devotion."

Iris has no idea what he means, but it seems to please him to talk. She sees Josephs and Marys, and Jesuses of all ages and humors. Abandoned over and over again, because imperfect, because unworthy?

The Master rails on, punctuating his pauses with caresses of his brush. "Painting holy subjects has always made a good living for painters! Though who among us doesn't fear being dashed into hell when we paint into a sacred scene from Scriptures some baby we see on the street, a woman we love, a man we admire?"

The Master becomes morose. "And besides picturing the blessed"—this in a sour tone, carping—"as a painter I catalog the corruption of the world! In staggering honesty. The misshapen, the unholy aberrations. The Girl-Boy of Rotterdam? I painted that cursed soul the year before it was stoned to death by the devout. I painted the Seven Stages of Plague, including the gray-green face of the unburied corpse. The hunchbacks, the split-skulls, Dame Handelaers with her horrible donkey jaw. The other side of revelation! Through that door, should you want to see. I'll unlock it for you. All the proofs of our need for God." He points his brush at the door and raises his eyebrows in a question.

Iris doesn't even dare to look at the door, much less ask for it to be unlocked. She doesn't want to see. She wraps her thin arms around her thin chest, and asks herself again: Where have we come to?

The Master turns back to his canvas. "And I'll paint that changeling child yet," he says grimly. "Haarlem's hidden beauty. More witness to the weirdness of this world."

Iris remembers the girl at the window, the girl who gave the toy to Ruth. She had asked if Ruth was a lost one, a changeling. Was Haarlem a haven for such goblin beasts? Iris had heard that from time to time a poor infant might be kidnapped from its cradle and replaced with a rotten, illish creature resembling it in looks alone. A changeling is said to be deficient of something essential, either memory, or sense, or mercy. Iris wants to ask the Master about the nature of changelings, and how to identify one, but he interrupts her thoughts, mumbling on.

"And even though I testify about the terrible human state, and its rescue by the sanctity of Jesus, what, what, what in this *annus dominus* are we brought to, we the laborers, the artisans, the cooks of linseed stew?" The Master throws his brush across the room. "They want *flowers*, flowers for commerce, beauty to sell as if it had its own sake! Why don't the dreamless Calvinists just go off to Constantinople? Why don't they join the pagan Mohammedans who rebuke the notion of portraying divinity in anything but Euclidean tiles of blue and gold? Or why don't I just take myself to the Spanish Netherlands and set myself up there? Where I can paint what I want, and keep food on the table as well?"

"Why don't you?" asks Iris, goaded from her shyness by his ranting.

"I love my home, and this is my home," he yells. "*Don't you understand that?*"

Iris doesn't answer. Home is hard to recollect already, usurped by that nightmare of torches, accusations, an escape in a flatboat over fields flooded with sea water, as the full moon blazed upon them like the eye of a vengeful judge. Her family had left home so quickly—who really knew if Jack Fisher was even given a Christian burial, or was he still drifting in the suck of the receding tides, a bloated corpse leaching his blood into the ruined crops?

"What, what is it?" says the Master, coming toward Iris, but she starts, and jumps away.

—a minor demon, sniffing the midnight air, on the hunt, chasing after them—

"No," she says, keeping it all unremembered, "no, *no*."

"Then if you won't say, out, out in the air, enough of my prattle; what do you care for the madness of an obsessed man? Go for flowers. Go with your enormous sister for flowers. Trot off and drag an armload of pretty weeds for me, so I can waste my time and feed myself."

He looks at Iris, then peers down into his brushes, splaying the bristles of one with his clean left thumb. "Bring me flowers, child," he says, more softly. "Out into the air with you. You look like a crone before your time."

Meadow

Schoonmaker—the Master—gives Iris a short knife. He tells her how to find the meadow. Iris helps Ruth put her wooden shoes back on, and she fits on her own pair. Then the girls clasp their hands and run.

Past the brewery with its rich active smells, down a lane that leads through a city gate. Out the gate, across a foul canal, up an embankment, through a mess of hedge, and then: the meadow. A few cows are companionably lowing. Ruth is scared of cows, so Iris flies at them and windmills her arms about, and the cows amble away without taking offense.

The sisters are alone for the first time since leaving their home in England. They aren't Dutch girls, no matter how well Margarethe had taught Iris essential words and grammar. But they're no longer English girls either, since home has been swept away from them. So for now they're merely alone, but together, as together as they can get.

Before the death of Jack Fisher, Iris and Ruth had been no farther from March than the next village over, and that only once, for a fair. What a disaster. The ale had flown too freely and the reticence that masquerades as Christian charity had collapsed. Men had set down their bowls of ale and taunted Ruth with a stick, saying they were hungry for bacon, and how much would the pig fetch? Iris had snatched that very stick and gone at them, and caused blood to flow, though even with dripping nostrils and split lips the men had fallen against each other in mirth. "The pig and the hound! The hound and the pig!"

The Fisher sisters had never gone to the market fair again. Nor had Iris told Margarethe or Jack exactly what had happened, for what would that mean? Just that Ruth would be kept closer to the hearth than ever. Iris has always thought this isn't right. Without question Ruth is an idiot, but she is not a pig.

Iris can't think about these things, though; when the memories threaten to return, she has to brush them away. She's left those things behind. She's left England behind, and all it means. Any cursed imp is left behind, surely, surely. But have they really arrived in Holland? Or did the boat go awry in the storm? Have they come instead to a place of bewitchment? Perhaps it only looks like Holland, and that's why the grandfather who was to take care of them is not in his house.

Don't be fanciful, says Margarethe's voice in Iris's mind. But Iris can't help it. The mysteries of this place! Whatever could the Girl-Boy of Rotterdam have been? Or Dame Donkey-Jaw? Or what about the changeling child? If this is no longer England, perhaps it's not Holland either. It's the place of story, beginning here, in the meadow of late summer flowers, thriving before the Atlantic storms drive wet and winter upon them all.

Iris lectures herself. Be commonsensical. Be good. Deserve the food you'll be fed tonight. She says, "So many varieties. What sorts does he want, do you think?"

Ruth plucks a daisy and holds it up.

"That's one, and a good one it is," says Iris, "he wants many. Here, Ruth, can you use this knife without stabbing your thumb? If you pull them like that, the leaves are crumpled. Make your cut down here—bend your knees, that's better. Yes, that's a good one. I don't need to approve each choice. All flowers are good ones, Ruth. Yes, that's another nice one."

Iris moves away as far as she dares, making sure that Ruth isn't alarmed. Then she moves farther still. She sees an abandoned apple tree at the edge of the meadow. Though it's crippled with age, there are boughs that can be used as a ladder, and she should be able to step from the apple tree to the limbs of the taller, weedy tree that grows next to it. Iris tucks her dark skirt into the band of her apron strings and puts her precious shoes at an angle against the trunk. She begins to climb.

She hadn't been able to see much of the world from the boat that had left from Harwich. Because of fright, hunger, and nausea, she had had to keep her head down on the creaking floor. Iris says to herself, I couldn't stand on the prow of the ship and track our journey to this odd place. But here, on the edge, on the margin, an aging tree is a stepping-stone to a taller tree, and from there . . .

Look one way, and beyond the lip of three or four more meadows is the broad gray ocean, crimped with white lines of water wanting to noise themselves against the dunes. From

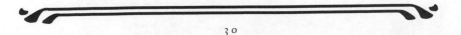

here the sea appears less monstrous than it had from the dock at Harwich. Then the light had been low, and the waves, close by, had pulled up weights of water, greasy, heavy, dark. Today the sky is hung with clouds random as sailing vessels, flat-bottomed and big-billowed, and the water seems smoothed, changed.

Look the other way, and she can peer above and beyond the leafy hedge, locate the mouth of the brown-blue Spaarne, and trace the river inland to the city walls. She can make out the buildings of Haarlem. Their smart chimneys, their tall facades imitating steps-and-stairs. There: the building she's come to know already as the Stadhuis, the town hall, with its green mountain of a roof. There: the Grotekerk—the Cathedral of Saint Bavo's—its stone spire the color of toasted bread, one angle pink and pockmarked in this light. A small ribbed dome, open to the winds, is perched up top like an airy onion.

Canals ring the town, joining to the Spaarne on north and south sides. Haarlem, or whatever world this might be, is a closed garden itself, of stone and glass and red roof tiles. Beyond, to the east, the occasional ouderkirk—as the Master told her—suggests a group of farmhouses, a crossroads, a ford. Iris looks to see some giant in the distance, some dragon laying a clutch of eggs. She finds an unraveling of smoke. It could be a dragon. It could be anything. "I think it's a dragon," calls Iris.

Ruth has forgotten her task already and sits chewing the stems of flowers.

Iris hasn't attended to flowers much. Things that grow have been their mother's concern: the roots, the herbs for their leaves and flowers, the flowers for their seeds, the many small snatches of sage, celery, and rue. Iris has overlooked them. But now she sees a nameless variety of wild blossoms. She can't call their names, in English or Dutch. After a few moments in an artist's workroom, she can see only flecks of gold, stalks of red and maroon, starry puffs of blue, stands of white, and all of it peppered against a glowing fold of yellow and green.

Iris says to herself: I will bring Margarethe here for the benefits to be coaxed from seedling, stem, and leaf. Margarethe is a mistress of the simples, and she can treat any ailment with an infusion or a plaster.

And there is Margarethe, striding back from the market already, a big fish shining from underneath her arm. Iris thinks her mother looks—from this height—ridiculous, her legs whipping out and her shoulders hunched over. She looks relieved.

"I see a wicked witch, and a cow that gives milk of pure gold," calls Iris. She decides she will drum up the courage to look at the paintings of the Master's demons and unnatural figures. All the secrets of the world are to be discovered and recorded!

A flurry of swallows on their way south. "Is that a school of fairies, flying from tree to tree?" she calls, to keep Ruth engaged. "Is that a changeling child I see?"

Below, Ruth smiles and doesn't bother to listen, a simple among simples.

Sitting
for
Schoonmaker

They come to know their patron and his tempers.

He wakes up as Schoonmaker and becomes, by grumpy effort, the Master. Mornings are full of muttered curses and swallowed blessings. Enthusiastically he washes himself, paying no attention to the modesty of maidens or widows. The Fishers have to huddle themselves in the kitchen yard until he calls for his laving water to be removed. Then, a cambric shirt pulled over his head at least, he berates Margarethe for every annoying thing: the thinness of the porridge, the hardness of the cheese, the grayness of the bread, the miniature nature of herrings.

Ruth plays with her windmill, the little thing grabbed from the beautiful girl in the house at the marketplace, until the Master roars for flowers. It doesn't happen every day—all field flowers don't die at once, no matter what he says—but it happens often enough.

After the first three or four trips, Iris doesn't need to escort Ruth to the meadow, though if the cows have frightened her Ruth comes home empty-handed. Iris sees, though, that the Master often doesn't look at the flowers Ruth brings. He stuffs them in a bucket and continues to paint the ones he already has, all the while quoting lines of Scripture, as if to punish himself by remembering what holy passion he is kept from because of the nonsense of flowers.

Iris loiters about the studio, trying to get up the courage to ask to see the paintings in the locked chamber of misfits. She is curious to see if he portrays imps and thwarties there. Here the Master paints flowers. "What are you bothering me for?" he mutters, not sounding very bothered.

"Have you ever seen a dragon . . . or a hell-imp?"

"The patron who doesn't pay his debt is a hell-imp . . ." What a middle-aged answer, and from one who claims to admire his own paintings of monsters and miserables!

She'll ask him tomorrow for the key to the other room. She will. She's always known about imps, and she wants to see one—not in real life (please God, no), but in a painting. That would be safe, and even wonderful.

But the tomorrow comes, and just as she is going to do it—she is, she is!—there's a knock on the door. "Caspar?" says the Master. "Come in!"

Nobody enters. "Iris, open the door, Caspar's arms must be heavy with presents for me," says the Master boisterously.

Timidly, Iris swings open the top half of the sectioned door. She sees nothing, but hears a knock on the bottom half.

"Be generous. Open the full door," says the Master.

She does. A horrible beast in a huge beard stands there, only as high as Iris's apron strings. It's a talking dog, or a bear cub? It growls at her: "Move aside, what are you staring at, you ugly thing?" A dwarf, a real dwarf. Iris is glad Ruth is in the meadow today. May she stay there safely until this creature leaves! "Where's the old goosander?" growls the creature, pushing in.

The Master seems unimpressed. "Who sent you here?" he said.

"For a half loaf of bread, I'll remove my smalls and show you how the barber tickled my gangrenous limbs with his knives," says the dwarf, who, it appears, is this short because he has no legs. He rocks forward, using his arms to swing himself. Then he rests on two little stubs at the base of his pelvis. They are fitted over with leathery patches laced up by thongs that tie over his shoulders.

"There's a female present," says the Master, "a girl."

"Oh, is it a girl?" says the dwarf. "Such a pretty face it has. I thought it was a monkey with an ailment. You're Schoonmaker, aren't you. Are you still drawing the likes of me?"

"You want me to pay you a half loaf of bread?" says the Master. "Bread is dear, and I've seen your like before."

"I've a handsome package of knobs and knuckles dragging along on the floor," says the dwarf, looking at his crotch.

"Get out," says the Master. "I'm interested in the varieties of the fallen, to be sure, but right now I'm busy with flowers. And I don't like your uncivil tongue when there's a girl present."

The dwarf looks at the Master's study of wildflowers. "You've gone from cataloguing us queerlimbs to portraits

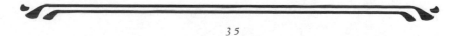

of—cow food?" says the dwarf. "Damn you, your reputation is riper than that."

"Margarethe, bring your broom," calls the Master calmly. "A talking clot of fur has rolled in the doorway. It wants removing, whether it knows it or not."

Iris loses her nerve about inspecting the gallery of misfits. When Ruth comes back, Iris tells her about the dwarf while Ruth sorts the flowers by height and lines them up on the windowsill for the Master to inspect. "Wonderful," he says. "So nicely arranged!" He doesn't move them. They dry and blow away the next day.

"Ready to draw you, before another crazy fish swims by to interrupt me," says the Master at last. Iris isn't sure she wants to be drawn, but a bargain is a bargain.

When the sun has moved to its proper place, the Master places Iris in a chair and composes her hands in her lap. He pulls the cap off her head. Tears start in her eyes. She is afraid he will undress her wholly. Her poor stick self isn't fit for it.

He misunderstands her concern. "The cap: *filthy*," he says, "and I'm not looking at you anyway, but at the shape of your head." He takes an hour making marks on the wall. She is supposed to focus on the marks, one after the other, while he keeps returning to his pad of paper and judging the cast of her eyes. By the time he's ready, the light has shifted. He curses her for her stubbornness and throws some flowers at her, and she runs into the kitchen, hiding her eyes—it isn't her fault!

"Cry a little bit if you have to. It's healthy to piss in the fire. But then back you go," says Margarethe, raising a spoon like a truncheon.

"He wants to draw a marble statue, not a person!" cries Iris.

"Then be marble for him, you fool," says Margarethe. "Be bronze if he wants it; be glass; be oak. Be what he wants, or we go hungry."

"He wants beauty," says Iris, rubbing her nose. "He has a hound, and he wants beauty."

Margarethe's expression is blank. At last she says, "Then be beauty. Make-believe it."

Iris gives a wordless cry of exasperation. If she had something to throw at her mother, she would throw it.

"He hasn't asked for—?" whispers Margarethe, making bosom-like drawings in the air with her left hand.

Iris shakes her head. Now, oddly, she's irritated. Clearly she's not *interesting* enough to be insulted in this way.

"I'm done drawing for the day, for the season, forever," cries the Master from the other room. He is stamping back and forth. "I'm trying to decide how to end my life, and you two nattering on like that, it breaks my concentration!"

"Begging your pardon," says Margarethe in a wry, placating voice. "I wouldn't want to interrupt some important thought."

He laughs. There is the sound of a piece of paper being torn. "We start earlier tomorrow, Iris," he says. "You will not elude me, whatever shyness you pretend to. I will fix your face on board without fail. My livelihood depends on it, and so does yours. Dry your eyes and hush your whimpers or I'll have to beat you."

Margarethe raises her eyebrows at Iris. Iris pouts. But by now they both know the Master is not one to beat children.

The next morning he is at work again, and Iris sits for him. He draws her face and hands and her shoulders. "Let your head sink more, advance your chin."

"My neck will ache unless I hold it straight."

"Do as I say."

She sits like a traveler at a campfire, imagining something at her back. Something that should have been left behind in England?—or some new monster, like the lewd dwarf, the Donkey Woman, something darker, inching nearer?

"What a complex wariness in your eyes!" he says.

Later: "Now, without a word of protest, without moving your eyes, your hands, your neck, push out your lower lip. I don't care how it makes you feel. Farther. That's good."

If he catches me, thinks Iris, will he catch what is at my back? That thing that I can't name? That thing I start from in my sleep?

"Is there really a changeling child in Haarlem?" she asks.

"I'm drawing your *mouth*. Close it!"

It's the worst torture anyone could have devised for her, to have to sit so still!

But, day after day, she sits respectably, clothed. And glad for it now. "Let me see what you have done with me," she says after the fifth afternoon. The lowering sun is pushing dusty golden light at the canvas, and she feels brave.

"There's no point," he says. "I haven't caught you. I'm not trying to catch you. I'm merely using you to suggest a